Ikenga Publishing Ltd would like to thank Sarah Khan, Vicky Garrard, Inmaculada Diaz-Ruiz and Ada Maya Uyanna-Diaz for their contribution in helping the book reach release phase.

Obi And His Curious Adventures

Written by Chinasa Uyanna

Illustrated by Troy Edwards

Ikenga Publishing Ltd

This book is set way back in the 1980s, which was before most people had the internet, smartphones and tablets. Throughout the book you may see and read things which are very different to how life is like nowadays.

Obi was born in London, England, in the United Kingdom. In London, the weather can be described as grey and wet. Obi was always aware that London was a busy place, with lots of different types of houses, shops, buildings, cars, buses and noises.

When Obi was four and half years old, his mum decided that it could be good for Obi to live for a short while with his grandma in another country. She felt that perhaps Obi might like learning new things in a new place.

It was time for Obi to say goodbye to London. Can you guess where he was going to?

Obi and his mum arrived at London Heathrow Airport, with a lot of excitement. Obi thought to himself, I wonder what my new city will be like, will it be as busy as London?

Heathrow was busy with lots of people travelling to different countries. Obi boarded the plane and was lucky to get a window seat. He stared out of the plane window and waved goodbye to the grey clouds.

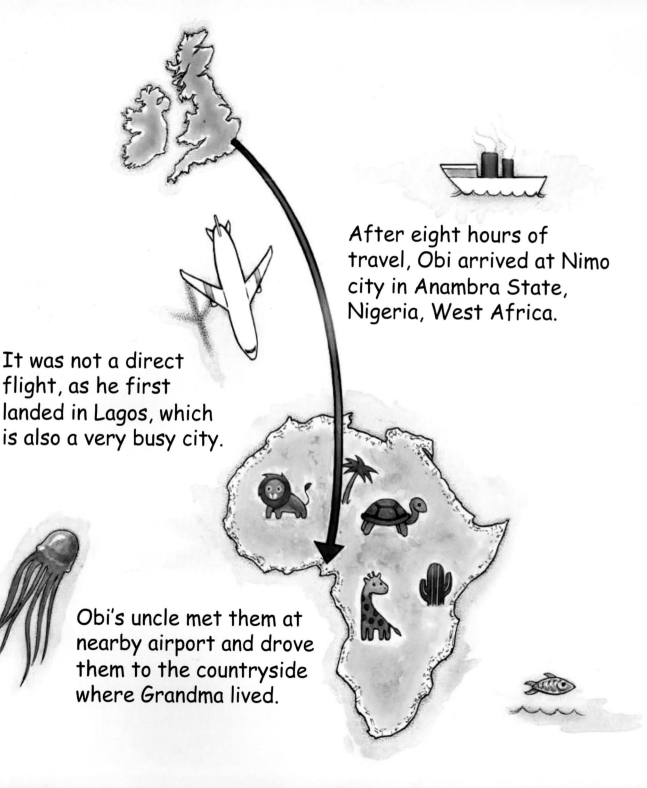

After eight hours of travel, Obi arrived at Nimo city in Anambra State, Nigeria, West Africa.

It was not a direct flight, as he first landed in Lagos, which is also a very busy city.

Obi's uncle met them at nearby airport and drove them to the countryside where Grandma lived.

When Obi arrived at his grandma's house, he was surprised to see such a big family waiting to greet him. He noted everyone was wearing flip-flops or sandals, t-shirts and shorts. It was also very sunny and there was a lot of open space. It was all very different from London.

"Kedu" Obi's grandma said to him. Obi asked his mum, "What does Kedu mean?" Obi's mum said, "It means 'How are you?' Say to Grandma Odinma, which means 'I am good'".

Obi responded, and his Grandma gave him a big hug. "Welcome to your new home," she said.

Chinelo Ike Uche Chika

Obi's cousins Chika, Ike, Chinelo and Uche all said "Kedu" at the same time.

Obi with confidence shouted "Odinma". They all laughed and hugged Obi. During the summer, Chika, Ike, Chinelo and Uche all stayed with their grandma, so the house became busy with lots of family.

As Obi went for a short walk outside, around his grandma's house, he noted a chicken and goat.

The chicken said to Obi, "Where do you think you are going?" Obi replied, "I am just walking around the house, as I am new here".

The goat said, "You must be Obi from London. Nice to meet you".

Obi asked, "So what is your name?" The goat replied, "I am Mr. Goat, and this is Miss Chicken". Obi said, "I must admit, I am not used to seeing chickens and goats at houses".

Miss Chicken laughed and replied, "Most houses here have chickens and goats. We also grow a lot of vegetables in our gardens.

Welcome to Nimo, I am guessing it's very different to where you are from". Obi responded "Yes, this is very different".

Chika arrived and said, "I'm glad that you have met Miss Chicken and Mr Goat, however it is time to introduce you to the sugar cane fields". Obi asked, "What is a sugar cane?". Chika responded, "I think it will be easier to show you, as we have a lot of things to do today. Come on London boy, let's go."

Chika and Obi arrived at the sugarcane fields. Obi looked around in awe. "What is this? "he asked, Chika replied, "Sugar canes". Would you like to try one?". Obi replied, "Try one, how do you do that?". Chika laughed, "Let me show you. I guess you are used to only seeing sugar in bags in London".

Chika broke one of the sugarcanes and showed Obi how to eat it. Obi copied Chika and said, "Wow, that is really sweet and delicious. Is this where sugar really comes from, from sticks?" Chika laughed and said, "Yes, we crush the sticks and the sweet juice that comes out gets made into sugar. Anyway, let me show you the lake now".

Chika took Obi to the lake, where Uche, Ike, Chinelo were
there with two extra buckets for Chika and Obi. Uche asked
Obi, "How was the sugarcane?" Obi said, "Delicious, hopefully
we get to go again tomorrow". Uche responded, "Well yes of
course, however first let's collect some water to take back to
Grandma's house. We will be using the water for general use at
home, like cleaning and cooking". Uche showed Obi how to
collect water from the lake and carry it on his head.

When the cousins arrived at Grandma's house, they all poured the
buckets of water into the well. Chika explained how a well works
to Obi. "The bucket is attached to a rope and is used to gather
water at the bottom of the well. The rope is part of a winding
system. When the bucket is full, a lever handle is wound to pull
the bucket back up". Obi found the well- system fascinating. He
said "I am looking forward to using this tomorrow. I have never
seen a well in London".

After dinner, it was time for Obi to go to bed. He was so tired especially after the long trip from London and all the different things he had done on his first day. Obi laid in bed and thought about all the new experiences from his first day in Nimo.

He tried to decide what the best part of his day was. If you had to choose for Obi, what event would you say was the best?

THE END......OR UNTIL
THE NEXT CURIOUS
ADVENTURE........

Let's check how well you know Obi and his curious adventures. READY for some questions?

QUESTIONS

1. What was the name of the city that Obi was born in?

2. How did Obi describe the city he was from?

3. How old is Obi?

4. Did Obi travel to East Africa, North Africa, South Africa or West Africa?

5. How long was the flight that Obi took?

Let's check how well you know Obi and his curious adventures, READY for some questions?

QUESTIONS

1. How many cousins did Obi meet when he arrived at Nimo?

2. What animals did Obi meet when he arrived at his grandma's house?

3. What did Obi taste when he explored a new place with Chika?

4. Do you think Chika was older or younger than Obi?

5. What did the children pour their buckets of water into when they arrived back at grandma's house?

6. Was it the sun or moon that was shining out of Obi's room when he was sleeping?

Ikenga Publishing Ltd is a small London based boutique publisher specialising in the production of creative works that references West African culture.

Text © Chinasa Uyanna. Illustrations © Troy Edwards
First published in UK in 2020 by Ikenga Publishing Ltd

20-22 Wenlock Road, London, England, N1 7GU

ISBN: 978-1-5272-6872-2

The illustrations was created in watercolour and then edited digitally.

Manufactured in UK.